William Bull Wright

The Brook

and other poems

William Bull Wright

The Brook
and other poems

ISBN/EAN: 9783337118815

Printed in Europe, USA, Canada, Australia, Japan

Cover: Foto ©Andreas Hilbeck / pixelio.de

More available books at **www.hansebooks.com**

THE BROOK

AND

OTHER POEMS.

BY

WILLIAM B. WRIGHT.

———•••———

NEW YORK:

SCRIBNER, ARMSTRONG & CO.

1873.

PART I.

———:0:———

THE BROOK.

THE BROOK.

I.

BRIEF the search until I heard him,
Sweetest truant at his play;
Such a soul of laughter stirred him,
Could not rest by night or day.
Brief the search until I found him
Gambolling, crumpling all his bed;
Woods and rocks, that loved him, round him,
And the brakes twined overhead.
As I came, away he sped
On fleet pearly feet of lightning
Just behind a rosy croft:
Flashing thence with sudden brightening,
Tossed his baby head aloft,

And with cries of merriment
Down the sombre forest went.

Madly merry elfin soul,
That peeps askance from silver bubbles,
Whose careless foot the tawny shoal
Plagues with fifty frothy troubles,
Where is thy birthplace, what thy goal?

From the mountain's stubborn womb,
See, he springs, a new-born creature,
Clothed with grace and of immortal feature.
From its jail of eldest gloom,
Lo, his naked spirit is set free,
And, drunken with his goodly liberty,
Romps and frisks the heavenly child;
And as a meteor wild,
His bright hair flung in flashing trail
Backward from his forehead pale,
Tiptoe upon nimble feet
He visits and he quits the sight,
An apparition fair and fleet,

Shaped of wonder and pure delight.
O joy, that from a thing so dark
There could be struck so bright a spark !

'Tis but the joyous quality
Of life, that pricks his heart with glee.
So blithe, so rash, he cannot guess
What burdens gather to oppress,
What world-old wrestlers, stanch and grim,
Sit by the wayside waiting him ;
Whose savage grapple without ruth,
Unlocks the tender joints of youth.
The child among his rattles,
What though he not forebode
The shock and din of battles
That wait him on the road !
Suffice unto the happy elf
The wonders of his present self.
What profit, though he knew that Fate
Already snuffed his track,
Yea, from behind his very back
Reached stealthy fingers to create

From the toys he breaks and idly scatters
Adamantine links of future fetters !

Yet offices of sovereign power
The gods have granted him for dower :
A sceptre ripens for his hand,
And mustering myriads wait for his command.
A kingly germ, that shall wax vast
And over many lands his shadow cast.
And old alliances and strong
To him by right of birth belong;
Treaties knit with cloud and sun,
That never will their bond outrun.
Fortunate the soul that greets him
Soft and kindly when he meets him.

What need has my sweet child of wings ?
He can out-trip all adverse things.
See his silver sandal flash,
So cunning-wise, though seeming-rash !
So soft to glide, so quick to flit,
What force can bind or intermit

The motions of his flowing wit?
In his mystic pace does dwell
All the speed of Neptune's shell,
All the stealth of Mercury's heel,
All the fire of Phœbus' wheel.
Languors dull or grosser slumber
Never stay his ramping limb:
The gods gave all their gayety
When they modelled him.
Playmates has he without number,
And oh the joy it is to see
Their games of utter jollity,
The graceful grapples, the pettish quarrels
Mixt with careless peals and blithest carols.
Oft his lithe athletic pranks
Scale the rampart of his banks.
Now he flecks with wanton spurt
The thicket's flower-broidered skirt;
Now with light malicious dart
He elbows all the sleepy sedges;
Quarrying now with spleenful art,
Caverns all his crumbling edges;

Now his clear thews plump and strain,
As with tug and might and main
He wrestles with the bulky ledges,
Who with thievish foot thrust out
Trip him headlong from his route.
But no boisterous hap or rude
Can repress his nimble mood.
Vanquished, he wears the victor's crown,
And, often thrown, is never down.
May'st dash him side-wise from the height—
Some god has taught him this fine sleight—
He will upon his feet alight.

Who could lure thee but to tarry
While he spake a word with thee,
Take in a net thy spirit wary,
Till it told its cause of glee ?
So oft thy humor veers and doubles,
I cannot guess thy will or reason,
Or thrid the tangle of thy mind,
That, never seeking, still does find ;
Drinks deep through every tingling nerve,

And thrills through each voluptuous curve

With dizzy transports of the season.

But when thy waves are crisped and curled

Against a lily or a pebble,

And all about thy woodland world

Echoes thy dainty-trilling treble,

Or when with airy leap and laughter

Thou dancest down the sloping shelf,

Trailing a hundred ringlets after,

I sometimes catch the sprightly elf,

Who cannot always hide himself.

A wisdom to thyself, a gladness,

It well beseems thee to disdain

The mortal's haughty scope of sadness,

The griefs that make our lives profane.

Oh glorious skein of sunlight

Fresh from the spindle of love divine,

Thou art to me a heavenly sign

To cheer, ennoble, and invite.

Something within me strongly pleads

To follow where thy splendor leads ;

I cannot doubt the path is right :

I give myself to thee to guide me,
Be thou my fate, whate'er betide me.

But what is this, and who is here?
What lovely child, so blithe of cheer?
Chanced it, that an amorous Vale,
Nymph-like lying in the sun,
Saw the fair boy come a-maying
Through the thickets one by one,
Hundred flowers stuck in his belt.
Quick through all her limbs she felt
Soft voluptuous tremors run.
She, his careless sport waylaying,
Snatched him up in eager arms,
In her fragrant bosom hid him,
Made him free of all her charms,
Would no tender liberty forbid him.
But no heat yet spurred the flood
Of his fresh and temperate blood.
Not yet the mystic seed was sown,
As far as Love he had not grown.
With fine frown and fairy pout

Tosses he to break from ward ;
More he wrestles to be out,
More the door is sweetly barred.
All his sighs and shrieks and hisses,
Double-pays she back in kisses.
If he coil himself to spring,
Tighter, warmer will she cling ;
With her leafy hair she blinds him,
Mazes him in its thick skeins,
And despite his rudest pains,
Well-nigh hand and foot she binds him.
Failing force, he beckons wit,
And to drowse her fierce suspicion,
Slowly feigns it to be well content
With her fire and throbbing blandishment.
While her ardors intermit,
While the soft gyves bate their hold,
Swift amain he bursts from prison,
And with Io Pæan bold
Zigzag skirts the level wold.

When from Nature's generous stock

Was fairer blossom born than this,
Around whom richer qualities
In sweeter order flock?
Opulent is childhood's hour;
'Tis he alone can give with grace,
And he alone can ask with power.
To the arch menace of his eye
And his half-imperious ways
Old Nature can no thing deny,
She grants him all he claims to own;
But the dear smiles that sometime light his
        face,
Bewitch the grandam to the bone;
Straight she unlocks her chest and brings her
        hoard,
And chooses him for heir of all, and lord.

And best it suits his bounteous heart and
        pleasure
To be royal-lavish in his measure.
Upon waste and fertile place
He sows the largess of his grace.

He, the son of myriad kings,
He, the heir of countless lands,
Wide his goodly treasure flings
To whoso asking stands.
But for his generous trust in her,
Nature her wayward worshipper
With tenfold measure will requite ;
Coins his harms to just and right ;
Reaps from his dear improvidence
Harvests of large experience ;
Husbands each squandered farthing of his
    dower,
And brings it back, changed to eternal
    power.

II.

O CUNNING baby Proteus, cover
Thy discourse with amorous art :
Aptly canst thou feign the lover,
And the sickness of the heart.

Hark, in the embowered land
Some courtly knight his dame is wooing ;
Polished the accents fall and bland,
Her lily favor proudly suing.
Low he bows his lofty state
To offer up the burning prayer,
And, like a broken pomegranate,
The fragrant soul of love is there.
Now the multitudinous vows
Chase each other from his lips,
Thick as 'neath his lady's brows
Gleam the golden-pointed lashes,

As the refluent blush that dips
Momently her cheek in flashes.

Thus the Lily hears him pray :
" Quit, O faery queen, the dryness
Of thy pensive solitude.
Wilt thou but forsake thy shyness
And take on another mood,
I will scoop a crescent bay,
Line it round with silk-soft foam,
Fan it with cool-rippling air :
Lo thy palace and thy home !
Torrid beam shall not impair
The fine tinct upon thy cheek,
Eavesdrop breeze shall never seek
To report Love's conference :
And no thing of loathsome sense,
Eft or toad, shall on thy sleep
Through the grassy lattice peep,
Lattice of thy bedchamber.
Clearest mirror will I burnish,   ·
Hide it where no wave can stir,

Where no prowling dust can tarnish,
No malicious breezes rove,
Heart-deep, heart-deep in the cove.
May'st the livelong rosy morning
At thy snowy toilet stay,
All thy saintly soul adorning
In its consecrate array."

But the Lily nodded nay;
And with nicely curious care
Pruned and plumed her petals fair.

Ah, childhood's vernal frost must thaw
In the warm summer of a larger law.
A new star spheres itself in view,
Whose beams are yeast along his veins,
That throng his heart with strange ado.
The surge, the dance, the pleasures and the
　　　　pains,
The fine alarm, the magic turbulence
Puzzle his thought and dally with his sense.
Now his chirp and frolic sleep,

Twilight vigils will he keep ;
Slips aside a meditative thing,
Talks with the stars and queries everything.

Too rude a breaking of the spell,
Fair spirit, this that thee befell.
As a colt that first time feels
Barbs that arm his rider's heels,
Forth he bolted, furious, blind
From the tempest in his mind ;
Wailed along his tortuous path,
Full from bank to bank of wrath ;
Shot through many a perilous flume,
Spat his ire in flakes of spume
Against the face of cliff and tree
That looked upon his agony.
Playing loosely with his fate,
Courts his doom with careless scorn,
In rude gorge or pool-set strait
Or on the wild crag's lowered horn.
Last, all dizzy with despair,
Topples headlong in mid-air

From a treacherous precipice ;
Bitter end of love was this.
Gored and mangled here he lay,
Steaming his life-blood away ;
Bitter end of love was this.

There a gray-beard hermit Glen
Lived his life recluse from men ;
Spelled in Nature's secret runes
And set his thoughts to holy tunes.
Virtues of every herb he knew
That nigh his bosky threshold grew :
No hurts so deep could well befall
But he would medicine them all.
Kind in heart, though harsh in look,
He stood beside the prostrate Brook,
Stooped and gently gathered him,
Gently, fondly, limb by limb,
Bore him to a grove hard by,
Plied his timely pharmacy,
Closed his rents and stanched his veins,
Set his limbs and eased his pains,

And as beauteous as before
Launched him from his coppice-door.

Riddle that he cannot read,
She must solve that did propound it;
From the fetter must be freed
By the finger that first bound it.
Comes the maid whose glances carry
In them Love's abounding presence,
His foot is caught, he can but tarry.
Sudden shocks of vague delight,
Tingling in through all his essence,
Sting his mind and gild his sight.
More his wit and courage fail him,
More he guesses what must ail him.
If her eyelids should uncover
Fires that answer to his own,
He moults his shyness and is grown
To the full stature of a lover.
Can then with ease in courtly phrases shine
And fledge his nimble parle with wisdom fine.
His lessons may the sage rehearse,

From him the poet thieve his verse;
Here orators may learn the perfect trick,
To bait their clauses with best rhetoric:
With logic brave he freights his speeding
　　　　　word,
And to convince, he asks but to be heard.

For his essence was too fine,
Scion of too proud a line,
Long to peak or deep to pine.
Mixed with him was too much glee,
All too full of youth was he,
Ah, too bent on love, to be
Prisoner long to anguish keen,
Or to nurse a tedious spleen.

Again his bright smile streams and gushes,
Turning all the world to joy,
And with myriad sunny flushes
Does his cheek and brow employ;
And around the swelling sweetness
Of his lips it darts and flies,

But it wins its rich completeness
In the dances of his eyes.

Stepping from a murky wood,
The quick starlight on his blood
Helps him to an amorous mood.
But warier than when he strove
To teach the Lily thoughts of love,
In the elbow of a shelf
Stops to groom and deck himself;
Taxing his wit to trim him gallantly,
In hope a faultless lover now to be.
Planning to be proudlier dressed,
Here he slips his woodland vest,
Mottled thick with flecks of shade,
And showing down its silver seams
Rents the envious rocks had made.
Wrought of ambers he loves best,
Now a burnished jerkin gleams
Bubble-buttoned on his breast;
Broideries of starry beams
Down its bosom shoot and twirl,

Laces spun of spotless foam
Wayward round its margent roam :
'Tis in sooth no vulgar churl.
Balanced here betwixt the rocks,
Now he combs and sleeks his locks,
Sidewise parted on his head ;
Locks in many a rippling curl
Down about his shoulders shed.
Then as softly forth he flows,
Dons his pebble-tinted hose ;
Seated on an eddy's whirl,
Buckles on his shoes of pearl ;
Then to horse ! and well-a-way !
Backed upon a current brown,
Ambles forth by grange and town,
Singing to right and left his roundelay :
Oho, was never seen a sight so gay.

Maids, that yet refuse to love,
Close the lattice now and shove
Deep the bolt along the groove.
Maids, that wait for Hymen's torch,

Hasten to the lamp-lit porch :
Let the beaming cestus rest
Soft below the heaving breast ;
Gorgelet, wristlet, let them shine,
On their snowy pillows sleeping,
And the satined slipper fine,
Coyly from its ambush peeping.
For a lover rides your way,
Will make ye grave or make ye gay.
Lo he comes, Love's throbbing star,
Heart to make or heart to mar ;
And his lips, Love's perfect bow,
Shoot words that kindle as they go.

What sombre pile is this we see
In the moonlight standing hoary,
So gaunt, so stern, it well might be
Famed in antique song or story ?
Round its towers the darkling vine
Clambering coils her leafy spire ;
Above it the primeval pine
Sweeps his memory-burthened lyre,

That still repeats the lofty strophes learned
When first the felloe of the heaven was turned.
'Tis the abbey of the vale :
Save the meek foot of contrition,
Naught can pass its sacred pale,
Or the snowy-plumed petition
'Scaping on its starry mission.
Here a band of Roses pray
To High God by night and day.
These, a spotless sisterhood,
Sweetly cloistered, live and brood
On the glories of their Lord
And the promise of His Word.
From an oriel in the green
One, the fairest, chanced to lean,
All her maiden bosom bare,
Forth upon the starlight air.
Lost in thoughts of piety,
Here she told her rosary,
Dewy beads, right out of heaven sent,
To grace her holiness and pure intent.

Spying her, Love's eager hunter
Thither spurred his course enamored.
As he galloped to confront her,
Merrily, merrily down the night
The thin hoof of his jennet clamored.
Better to bewitch her sight,
Lightly proves his gay manege :
No Parthian or Numidian feat
But he the wonder could repeat :
Pricks his steed to headlong rage,
Then with deftly fingered snaffle
Will his foamy urgence baffle.
Shifting aye his limber pace,
Curvette, pirouette, capriole, caracole,
Down he sweeps with gallant grace.
So bold a rider, a form so fair—
What marvel the maid should midway stop
In her maze of Aves, and let drop
The golden filament of her prayer !

Thus he frames his cunning plea :
" Well love I the hopes that gladden

Hearts that stagger, sorrow-laden :
Dear the fount whose lustral rain
Purges off the worldly stain :
Sweet the gloom of holy cell,
And christened fancies that there dwell :
Yet one thing hateful is to me,
The pride of perfect piety.
Sweeter than thy miserere,
Joy whose warblings never weary ;
Wiser than thy credos old,
Faith that never has been told ;
Chaster than thy barren vows
Warm thick oaths that Hymen knows ;
And holy as thy frigid rites
Love's hallowed days and fervid nights.
Shafts thou wouldst seal up in quiver,
Love has thieved and shoots at me ;
Hurts they scatter can be never
Wholly salved unless by thee.
Maiden, bate thy virgin edge
And accept Love's privilege.
What the kindly Life permits us,

Well to welcome, best befits us.

World is ours, let us not slight it ;

Dark, we have Love's lamp to light it,

Cold, Love's hearth is good to warm it,

Evil, Love can best reform it.

Come, within my bosom nestle,

While with stubborn things I wrestle.

Every thrust of mortal harm

Will I parry with sure arm.

Year may wax and year may wane,

We will scud the flowery plain,

Above, the skyey flag unfurled,

Around, the softly murmuring world,

To the land that Love likes best,

And bowers where he makes his rest.

There to thy divine Ideal

Will we rhyme our Hymeneal :

Heaven, whose sweets thou pin'st to prove,

Will grow round us while we move ;

God thou findest now so fair,

We will meet him everywhere."

The sweet Rose sadly shakes her head,
Shakes her head, and with a sigh
Thinks of Him that for her bled;
And with rapt and earnest eye
Points her finger up on high.
A zephyr ferries to his ear
The soft freight of her whisper clear,
" My bridegroom lives above the sky."

Still and deep, his bitter sorrow
Could no help from anger borrow.
Slow dismounts and steals with heavy foot
Where the mud-bound osiers thickest shoot.
Hoary wood and solemn shadow
Strive to lull his aching blood;
But no balm could stanch his mood
Or suck the low threne from his strain,
Till his sister, the green Meadow,
Laughing, caught him to her breast,
Laughing, soothed him and caressed,
Soothed, caressed, and charmed his pain.

My darling pet, what heart can chide
Thy elfin angers, thy wayward pride ?
Wrought of tuneful impulses,
Dainty shocks and fairy sallies,
Who can fathom or express
This quaint soul that with thee dallies ?
To repel or to caress
Swift as light and sure as thought ;
Rich in weird and golden chances,
Born of protean phantasy,
Rich in blithe or solemn dances,
Such as never yet were taught
In choric chant or mystery,
Round thy stirring lips the air
Leaps and thrills with melody,
Round thy feet the meadows wear
Flowery vests of light and glee.

Lightened of his load of woes,
To the homely Spearmint flows ;
Whispers in low silver tone,
Suited to love-theme alone,

" O sweet lady, lowlier bend,
Till with warm and foamy lips
One rich kiss of Love I send
Glowing to thy purple tips."
Then with amorous fervency,
And a gush of piteous sighs,
Up he flung the brilliancy,
Of his wild and ardent eyes,
And with amber-veinèd arms
Would have clasped her drooping charms.
So impetuous is his suit,
That soul of fragrance listens to 't,
Pities his heart-wrung distress,
Loves his valor and his grace ;
Comes and kneels and fondly tips
The pale sorrow of his face
With her incense-breathing lips,
And returns his warm embrace.
He with passionate intent .
Pauses there his glittering trail,
Sips the odorous freightage sent
Under convoy of the gale,

Till their hearts were wholly mingled,
Each the truth of each did prove.
" From all flowers have I singled
Thee to be my queen of Love,"
Sang the glad contented Brook,
As his shining curls he shook
And down the vale his saunter took.

Whatever Beauty has of power,
Of favorite law or fond creation,
Supplies unto thee hour by hour
The grace and spirit of thy fashion.
And I count it not a blame
That thou never art the same.
Let the world not suck the hues
From the iris of thy soul,
Put to meaner forms of use
Elements so dear as these,
Unsettle from their native pole
Thy revolving sympathies.

Who so kingly in his giving,
3   .

As who gives with lover's hand ?
Spending more, the more receiving,
And by loss his fortunes stand.
He will melt his sceptre down
In brooches for the maid he loves,
Pluck the jewels from his crown
To trim her bosom as behooves,
Quarry will his very throne
To pave her journey when she moves :
Having Love, can spare the rest :
Whoso loves, is at his best.

III.

HAVE ye seen upon the steep
The young minstrel with his lyre?
He can teach to laugh or weep,
He can kindle thoughts of fire.
In his cap white plumes of mist,
By cool matin breathings kissed,
Jauntily hither and thither play.
Loosely round his shoulders thrown,
Hangs his cloak of glittering spray,
'Twixt whose folds, asunder blown,
In faint shy colors may be traced
The belt of iris, whose light zone
Sleeps upon his slender waist.
Over him the monstrous clifts
Into battlement and tower
Each his savage height uplifts.
Here some fallen antique power,

Exile from Heaven's supremacy,
Nurses Olympian phantasy ;
Will with sombre grandeur keep
Show of primal dignity.
He, of midnight soul deform,
Evil, desolate and gaunt,
Clothed with thunder and with storm,
Loves the rocky waste to haunt.
Him the Brook with music strong
Hopes to charm by power of song,
To lure his presence from its lair
And memories that feed despair.
Now in wild fantastic gushes
Round his clarion tones he throws,
Now in soft melodious hushes
Deep and still his passion flows :
Now, a rhapsodist inspired,
He chants in lofty epic measure
Of martial heroes, glory-fired,
Of Battle's pomp and shock and seizure.
When this stately mood does ebb,
Warbles he, a tender lyrist,

Finely spins a golden web
Of the fancies that lie nearest ;
Sprightly ditties, elegies
Of slow-thoughted melancholy ;
Trills a lark in summer skies,
Or becomes a cuckoo wholly.

But no rhythmic force sublime,
Subtlest feats of harmony,
To that gloomy soul can climb
Or entice his amity.
Dark and sullen stands he ever,
Wrapt in glaring desolation,
His hard forehead changing never
Its supreme unbending station ;
But the adamantine scorn
Wrinkles there from morn to morn.

In fierce farewell the angry brook
With arms of spume defiance shook ;
Flung high his lyre, that murmured still,
Against the frowning of the hill,

And in a dark-stemmed hazel glade
Sheathed his straight and gleaming blade.

Knows the Bard by love, by love,
What his hands shall stir to fashion,
Swoops around it, broods above,
Handles it with plastic passion :
Pours the marrow of his mind
Through the thing he would create ;
May be little, may be great,
Must be perfect in its kind.

When Love comes piping up the road,
The Muse, know well, lags just behind ;
The blithe eyes of the merry god
Roll rhythmic billows through the mind.
He in whose soul the gods have planted
The holy kernel of sweet song,
Must strive and strive, till he has chanted
The numbers that to him belong.
At first, a very babe in verse,
He totters through his timid line ;

Some homely things he may rehearse,
Some awkward syllables combine.
Older, he flies a ballad light
Upon the breeze of sweet romance ;
Heroic things his heart entrance ;
His phrases clash as knight with knight
His metres gallop to the fight.
Anon he roves, a hunter bold,
Up and down by wood and wold,
The bow of fancy strives to tame,
And all things are his game :
Or the proud falcon of his song
Dismisses on his forage airy,
Where, circling slow on pinions strong,
Beauty sails, the perfect quarry.
Works anew the fiery leaven :
Now a warrior brave and liege,
The gods themselves 'scape not his siege.
Against the sapphire walls of heaven
He sets the ladder of his rhyme,
And lightly mounts, intent to climb
As far as to the starry chime.

The eastern gable of the sky
Trickled with crimson down its tiles,
And wraith-like down the cloudy aisles
The moon slipped from the morning's eye :
And the dear bird that daily laves
His coat in saffron matin waves,
Up and down, at random whiles,
Began to build his proper note,
Angling by chance a mimic trill
Out of clear brook from alien throat.
Just where a virginal fair hill
Gathered the selvedge of her gown
From marsh-sunk meads, I paused to fill
My soul with sweetness that fell down
From the regarmented pure skies.
Lo from the hillock's dewy crown
He hastened, carrying in his eyes
All the bright dawn ; a bounteous store
Of hopes and golden auguries.
Their lordly valors ran before,
Making the world smooth for the way
Of this child-seeming conqueror.

Me sees he not : his glances play
About the eyelids of the morn,
And in them sweetly stand at bay
Such stars as never yet were born
On any sky, and from them stream
Soft rays of beauty, swift rays of scorn.
As one a fountain's silver gleam
May shiver with a pebbly bead,
So on his rapt translucent dream
Fell my rude words :

         "What strenuous need
Sets thus on fire thy agile pace ?
Pray curb the proud pomp of thy speed,
Fair Brook, and bait thy limbs a space,
And teach me of thy courtesy
What thing of grandeur or of grace
Tows thee in its bright wake ? "

              And he
Drew in the scouts of his wild eyes
From heaven's sapphire bastionry,
Saying, "A plume of splendor flies
Ever before me ; in its beams

The clear chart of my footing lies."
But when I strove with banter rude
To prick the bubble of his mood,
Saying, " No gracious thing it seems,
That one awake should still pursue
The flying feet of his own dreams,"
With scorn his ripples flashed and curled,
As back my trivial taunt he hurled :
" The rabble blows its trump through you.
The man that marries his own tongue,
That should be troth-plight to the True
And ever noble, chaste and young,
To stale spent words that haunt the street,
He does himself eternal wrong.
Get sight of it : once seen, 'tis sweet."
Therewith he turned his splendid head,
And stirred the rudder in his feet
For passage.   But I straightway said,
" These words were hatched upon the lip,
No deeper : I too have been led
By such light films, too fine to trip
A gnat's foot.   Prithee, gentle elf,

Sing me some history of thyself:
To greet with friendly speech behooves
    thee,
Every soul that wholly loves thee."

Just then the Morning's ruddy palm
Began to smooth his ringlets bright,
To lay his sudden heat, and calm
His quickened veins in baths of light.
Anon he swept his hand across
The crystal sinews of his lyre,
Set their chime to rhythmic laws
And tamed their wayward fire.
As round some warrior, that comes back
From toilsome wars with pomp and glory,
The people flock, and clog his track
And whisper his proud story,
So thick the varied numbers throng:
All young and lovely forms of sound
In quick procession gather round,
As with sweet proëmial pauses,
In rich frequence of melodious clauses,

He moves in triumph brave along
Towards the stately arch of song.

Through his million veins are poured
The splendors of the heaven whence he fell.
Wise above his thought is he :
Deep things he has to tell
To such as with a swift dexterity
Can aptly gloss his tangled word.
To an eternal song he frames his dance,
And urges his advance
Through numbers, motions intricately woven.
No pedant's eye avails to scan
The tumult of his foaming line,
Whose music owns a rule divine
To ears that once have caught the plan.
His notes so delicate and fine
My rudely fingered stop would crumble ;
Only some easier tones I twine
To wreathe my homely line.
But, ah, the strength, the scope, the vision,
The naive detour, the cadence sweet,

What bard could in his rhyme imprison,
Or bind with a melodious fetter
The prance of these fine feet!

" Whence I come or whither I go,
I little question, for well I know.
What I am, 'tis joy to be ;
Laughter is my vesture,
And a god of revelry
Beckons in my gesture.
I love my proper dæmon well ;
Summons he, I haste to follow
Through balmy grove or grassy dell
Or mountain's tempest-haunted hollow.

" Only to the sober eye
The gods withdraw the curtains of the sky.
Pressed from an immortal vine,
Temperance is eternal wine.
Who drinks my liquors chaste and cool
May slight the Heliconian pool :
He has no need to steal a sip

From Hafiz' bowl, or bathe his lip
In honey pressed from Pindar's comb,
Or taste of Bacchus' philtered foam,
Or filch from Chaucer's bounteous grace
Some liquid, limpid, purling phrase.
He shall take with heavenly sleight
In springe of couchant rhyme
The holy syllables, that in their flight
Skim the meads of Time,
And sometimes tarry for a night.
Lark-like they warble sweet and clear
Up and down the bustling sphere ;
Happy he that skills to hear
Their feathery oarage light.

" Wide waves the harvest of sweet song,
Long since the gods have sown the seed :
Thither a thousand reapers throng,
But since the flinty stalks grow strong
Their sickles clip the easier weed.
Strives one with sweat and sober heed
And limbs that ache and hands that bleed

To sheave some score of stems,
The dear wise world, that loves the weed,
His heavenly task condemns.

"I know ye folk of birth and death,
And of what troublous stuff is spun
The feeble tissue of your breath.
I know your fashions every one ;
Your gait and features smooth or grim,
From him that wakes a raw papoose
To him whose tongue his parents loose
With babbling of a Christian hymn.
Well I know the woman's wail,
Who comes, like bird from forage-quest
With loaded bill unto her nest,
And finds her tender chitlings dead :
What beak hath brought ye death instead ?
Sorrowful numbers flock around,
Earth-born ditties full of tears,
The loss, the cross, the myriad fears
That sting and madden and confound.
Ye call the law of your own fate

Rough to the feet, unfriendly, cold,
But if the heart be free and bold,
It turns to beautiful and great.
Come forth and love it, and 'tis thine,
Works like a strong man by thy side ;
But dodge or weep or fall supine
Or take a lesser thought for guide,
The pebble of the rill
Has power to kill.

" For my frolic lyre refuses
Fellowship of moping muses.
Touched by a single note of pain,
His simple chords would crack atwain.
He to Heaven is strongly sworn
To sound the hymns of utmost joy
And things of joyance born ;
Pledged to a large exulting song,
To which no sombre tones belong,
That, riding high above man's narrow state,
Perfect and full and beyond sweetness sweet,

Teaches the maiden stars their heavenly gait
And those soft flashings of their silver feet.

" In Beauty's light forever,
In Beauty's living light I rove.
Through darkling gorge, on open heather,
Be it fair or windy weather, `
Surest guide and amplest giver,
Evermore she shines above.
Never yet has she forsaken
The child once to her bosom taken ;
But as the hen-dove, brooding, covers
The chirp and flutter of her young,
With warm resplendent wing she hovers
O'er those that to her fold belong.
From her dear breasts the milk I draw
That feeds me with eternal youth :
She is the spirit of my shifting law,
The gage and warrant of my truth.
She is the musical blood of my song,
The sensitive marrow of my note ;
She shaped the syllables for my tongue,
4

She spun the allegro in my throat.
She kneaded and fashioned and burnished my
        limbs,
Not to be wounded by aught that impinges,
And, subtler than fins of a fish that swims,
She hid in my joints their mystical hinges,
And taught me my ever unwinding pace,
Fresh and capricious and fertile in grace.

" Engarmented in her own splendor,
With severe and orderly motions
Stilly charioted,
Myriad lures and charms attend her,
And the slumbering azure oceans
Boil and foam to her spiritous tread.
With sweet ineffable laughter,
With cunning resistless beckonings,
With musical coercive reasons,
Wooing, persuading, seducing, enchanting,
She draws the hoary firmaments after,
Set to wondrous tunes and perfect seasons.

With bounding eagerness and breathless pant-
      ing
The fair young Suns leap forth in her wake
From the thick abysses of night,
And passionately palpitating,
Haste the virgin Moons with bosoms bare,
From their half unfilleted hair
Shaking the pale white blossoms of light.

" Likewise for me she brims
A bowl of her liquor divine ;
The arches of my limbs
Are drunken with the wine ;
Round the curves of my feet and thighs
The liquid madness flies.
Through and through with her barm am I
      lightened,
In and out with her glory brightened."

IV.

ALONG the eastern border gray
The night holds skirmish with the dawn,
And that strong star, whose fearless ray
Closest scouts the marching Day,
Has slowly from his watch withdrawn,
And many a far-flung crimson spear
Quivers in the cloudlet's breast,
As o'er the margin of the sphere
Lifts the Morn his haughty crest ;
And wide and near the lazy land
Fumbles with slumber's easy band,
While drowsy sounds in wood and field
From dreaming throats are faintly pealed.
Starts the nigh-belated swain,
As the prying ruddy beam
Cuts the tendrils of the dream
That tightly hugs his heavy brain.

The smoke climbs upward through the thatch,

The housewife lifts the early latch,

And standing on the door-sill sees

The thick dews winking in the trees,

What time the flapping chanticleer

Winds afar his horn of cheer,

And every bird of blithesome note

Fingers light his woodland oat ;

And the herdsman's whistle shrill

Stirs the laughter of the hill,

As through the meadowy mists he strides ;

Issuing from whose purpled tides

Towards the grange the sleepy kine

Reluctant trail their straggling line,

Whose burthened udders, as they pass,

Spill their rich streams on the grass :

And swinging light in either hand

The cedarn pail with well-scoured band,

The maid hies briskly down the lawn

With gathered sleeve and skirt updrawn,

And loose braids 'scaping from her hood,

Carolling in her matin mood

Some silly stave too weak to hear
But for its honest heart of cheer ;
Since in her breast, as everywhere,
Is manifold delight to spare.
Anon the yoke's laborious beam
Is locked upon the broad-necked team,
The farm-lad cracks his wanton thong,
The huge wain lumbers loud along,
Where the clustered haycocks steam
In the morning's simmering beam,
And striding heart-deep in the math
The mower lays the dewy swath,
Or rings with bantering rifle clear
A challenge to his stanch compeer.
And everywhere the human hand
Reaches for its proper tool ;
Since those whom Nature puts to school
Learn the rough eternal rule,
Who best can work, he shall command.

But fairest of the laboring throng
Is he that feeds my feeble song.

Bouncing from his pallet spread
Among the roots of fragrant larches,
Now he shows his welcome head
Through the forest's leafy arches.
Shalt not alway frisk and carol,
Must be harnessed with the rest,
And put off thy gay apparel
For a homely work-day vest.

Love-time is over, and too long
The muse has. dipped on wayward wing,
Henceforth the lyre must freight its string
With burdens of a graver song.
Since from every earth-born soul
Fate severe exacts his toll.
A yoke sits on the sunbeam's neck,
The moth finds chores about the field,
The zephyr tugs his sightless trace,
Fairest things must service yield.

Garbed in modest homespun suit,
Stiched of lilies' dappled leaves,

From the busket's dewy eaves
He hastes with serious mien and mute,
And that sweet feature of content,
Labor's richest ornament.

Towering past the jutting hill,
Stands the huge meal-whitened mill,
Asleep through all the maze of art
Coiled within its cumbrous heart.
Now unto his task he springs ;
Against the stubborn wheel he flings
His shining strength, and dares to seize
The mighty felloes in his hands ;
Against the paddles' massy bands
Firmly plants his stalwart knees.
His muscles swell, his breast expands,
He bows, he tugs, he heaves amain
With one prolonged resistless strain :
Straightway the moaning monster knows
The haughty master he must serve,
And quivering with reluctant throes
Swings upon his sluggish curve.

The wakened mill is all astir
With creak and shriek and whiz and whirr,
The leathern band begins to move
Down the pulley's slippery groove ;
The thick cogs sink their fangs of steel
In the sockets of the wheel ;
And swiftly turns with muffled moan
The upper on the nether stone.
Pacing round the mealy floor,
And watching through the rush and roar
The perfect play of every part,
The Miller gladdens in his heart ;
His eyes with happy lustres twinkle,
He laughs through every dusty wrinkle.

Spirit, my fancies wild and crude,
Too lamely hint the thing thou art ;
All images are over-rude
To shadow thy mysterious heart.
Yet I through many forms of being
Intent to find the steadfast soul,
Catch often type with type agreeing

To point to one unchanging goal,
Find faintly mirrored in a part
The features of the perfect Whole.

Though flitting thus from mood to mood,
None dare name thee false or slight,
For one divine similitude
Pervades each frolic form and gesture,
One beauteous soul of love and light
Peeps quaintly through the changing vesture.
Simple art thou, candid, clear,
And what the inmost heart intends
Does in the noble eyes appear,
And with thy merriest motion blends
A kind of reverence and fear.
Albeit thy wanderings are far,
And thy mazes Gordian-twined,
Thou canst never fail nor err
From the fixed counsel of thy mind.
Since beneath thy crystal scales
Lives the spirit of all beauty,
And through all thy change prevails

The one golden law of duty.
So while life deepens in his strain,
Confide in what the Spirit sends,
Sure pilot he, through loss and pain,
To happy havens, glorious ends.
Fare thee beautifully ever,
Wayward child of mystic motion,
Till thou touch some greater river
And the pulses of the ocean.

V.

WHO yonder turns his furrowed face,
Priest-like, and clothed with priestly grace,
Towards the sunset's fading rays ?
The peaceful heart, the faith serene
Shine in his venerable mien.
Benign, a gracious thing to greet,
His white beard flowing to his feet,
Here he stands at close of day,
And sheds an affluent benediction
On every soul that comes his way.
Up to his knees a monstrous bowlder,
That erewhile roughly charioted
Some Titan glacier from his polar bed,
Thrusts amain a swarthy shoulder
Midst the myriad-eddying foam.
This is his altar : here he pours
His solemn vesper sacrifice,

And with full voice adores
Eternal Truth, eternal Beauty,
Eternal Love beyond the skies.
All pastoral forms, both rude and fair,
Flock up the sacred rite to share.
The maiden brakes, in linkèd band,
Crowned with flowery fillets stand :
Comes every tree of stalwart limb,
And every trunk of aged bough ;
And many a crag of feature grim
Lowly bends his dusky brow ;
And ruddy knolls in tumbled throng,
Grouped about the meadowy plain,
Repeat the sacred evening song
From dell to dell in soft refrain.
He is their organ, he their voice,
Through him they grieve, through him re-
        joice ;
Himself the anthem that adores,
Himself the offering that he pours,
Himself the incense that arises,
And the strong prayer that heaven surprises.

The year moves to its sad decline,
A dull gray mist enfolds the hills,
The flowers are dead, the thickets pine,
In other lands the swallow trills ;
For since they stole his summer flute,
The moping Pan sits stark and mute ;
The slow hooves of the feeding kine
Crack the herbage as they pass,
The apples glimmer in the grass.
And woods are yellow, woods are brown,
The vine about the elm is red,
Crow and hawk fly up and down,
But for the wood-thrush, he is dead ;
The ox forsakes the chilly shadow,
Only the cricket haunts the meadow.

The feast is ending, the guests are going,
In bands or singly they quit the board ;
The torch is paling, the flutes stop blowing,
The meat is eaten, the wine is poured.

The warlike game of life is over,

The lists are closed, and hushed the field,
The weary warrior draws the cover
Across his battered shield.

What sombre metamorphosis,
Tell me, fantastic elf, is this?
And has dim age waylaid thy grace,
Stolen the dimples from thy face,
Set a fetter on thy mirth,
And touched thy bounteous heart with
            dearth?
The languid step, the weary eyes,
The feeble voice too well betoken:
Lamed are the wondrous energies,
And half the frolic spirit broken.
There is no laughter on his cheek,
His riant gambol is grown meek,
Yet are his shadowy depths intense
With some transcendent influence.
For no disasters can destroy
Thy secret hope, thy lofty joy,
The faith that neither comes nor goes,

Wavers not in any wind,
But with a consecrate repose
Ever clearly burns and glows
In the heart and in the mind ;
Through the spirit's lattices
Streams upon the common air,
Makes the stars appear more fair
And doubles upon evening skies
The loveliness they wear.

In thy still features is expressed
Mute rapture and a supplication,
A perfect peace, a heavenly rest,
The golden calm of holy passion.
It touches me with sweet surprise,
Transcends and startles and abashes,
As couched in this uncheerful guise
Thy deeper nature on me flashes.
Happy for thee, but most for me,
That to this spot I followed thee !
To read the simplest heart aright,
Must turn the leaf whereon is writ

The thing it prays for day and night.
Best judge is he that has the grace
To spy behind its shifting wit
The temple where it loves to sit,
And by the light upon its face
Divine the eternal type of it.

From her eyry in the north
The white-winged Winter screaming swoops,
Drives her talons in the earth,
And binds the land with frosty hoops.
The thin blood of the halting Brook
She curdles with her bitter look,
Locks in icy gyves his feet
And cuts his flesh with barbed sleet.
With weary back and head depressed
And long beard frozen to his breast,
He toils to draw his staggering flood
To the covert of a wood.
But see, he starts, he pricks his ear,
He claps his aged hands for glee :
Ah ! closer now he seems to hear

5

The music of the eternal sea,
The haven and the perfect goal
To which the tides of being roll.
He shouts, he snaps his icy chain,
His spirit from its burden frees ;
Light as a roe he skims the plain,
Swift as a dart he flees.
The little earth of death and birth
Is fast behind him falling,
And stronger, clearer, louder, nearer,
The awful Deeps are calling.

Time, the tamer, puts his bit
In the strong man's mouth :
His hirelings in the saddle sit
And quell the blood of youth.
Time, the herdsman, turns his years
To pasture on his vernal cheek ;
Ploughman, through his feature steers
A stealthy share in grooves oblique ;
Reaper, he with sickle cleaves
From his eyes their burning sheaves ;

With flail from his adventurous heart
He threshes all the bolder part;
With fan he winnows from his lip
The airy laugh, the winged quip.
Upon his brow the quill of care
Begins to write a sober page,
And through its raven warp his hair
Admits the hoary woof of age.

The rumble of the world's loud course
Ebbs from his inattentive ear,
The wine of youth has spent its force
And leaves his spirit clear.
Now solemn themes his thought employ,
He sits on Nature's temple-stair,
Walks by immortal founts of joy
And haunts the tripod of sweet prayer.
Forebodings bright to him are given,
His faith burns like a sun,
And up the shining porch of heaven
His hopes like couriers run.
Upon his lips ripe Wisdom lays

Her purple clusters forth,
His words are fragrant with sweet praise
And glad with holy mirth ;
And life's tumultuous dithyramb
Changes to an eternal psalm.

PART II.

———:o:———

SONGS AND STUDIES.

SONGS AND STUDIES.

CHANCE stalks of Song, for which no plough-
    share ripped
The belly of the glebe, of which the seed,
No planter measuring out his careful pace
Sowed through the chinks of the quick-
    swinging palm,
But rather random-strewn by grace of wind
On pastures where the Fancy loved to browse—
Nor yet far off, but bordering close the broad
Well-ordered seed-field of laborious thought—
These, loosely gathered in a little sheaf
For him to thresh that has the will, I bring.
Some wild brake-buds, for fragrance or for
    tint
Culled by the captious finger;—now, to me,

Half-withered   rhymes   that   only   faintly
    breathe
The happy perfume of their earlier sweet ;—
Some trefoil-blossoms, plain enough, and yet
No heart was mine to slight them utterly,
So thick they thronged and clung about my
    feet ;
These, as a maid that to her lover sends
Some sober gift, will stick it round with
    flowers,
These have I tucked within the girth, in hope
To lay a beam or two of transient grace
Across the homely fardel that I bring.

THE STRAYS.

THE budding maid, not half a flower,
  When first the warbling days of June
Build nests about the household bower,
  Loves to unlatch her little shoon
And wade and paddle in the grass
  From matin to the glare of noon.
The tickled soles in frolic pass
  Their wonted range ; she slips along
From mead to mead, a truant lass.
  , Gliding, she purls, a brook of song,
Tripping, she chirrs, a happy dove,
  Dancing, she shouts, a bacchante strong.
Crowfoot and buttercup for love
  She gathers, but the fingers fair,
Though bursting, cannot pluck enough.
  She thrusts them, blithesome, in her hair
Longwise and crosswise, to her taste,
  And since her hands have yet to spare,

She trims her bosom and her waist;
    Then looping up in graceful fold
Her span of apron, fills in haste
    Its fairy hollow with the gold,
And, gazing sadly round her, sighs,
    Nigh weeps, because it will not hold
All the bright meadows in her eyes.
    Anon she smiles, in thought to please
Her mother with a dear surprise,
    And sitting plaits upon her knees
A chaplet; round it throng to sip
    A choir of splendor-drunken bees.
Right homeward then with trill and skip
    She gambols, dangling from her arm
The sweet grace of her workmanship;
    And, entering, springs with kisses warm,
And clambering to the mother's breast
    About her temples girds the charm;
Who lightly chides the foolish quest,
    The truant prank, the hoiden play,
But sits for secret gladness dressed
    In those poor weeds the summer's day.

O darling maid !—And shall I chide

   The wayward muse, the elfin stray

That brings from brook-marge and hill-side

   Flower-foam and waifs of woodland rhyme ?

Not I : be not the grace denied

   To wanton in her honeyed prime,

If faintest foretaste but abide

   Of sober thought in riper time.

SONGS IN SOLITUDE.

THE dreamy current of the day
   Drifts past me to the breathless west,
The hills are wrapt in autumn gray.

   Feathers of mist, plucked from the breast
Of one white cloud, a languid breeze
   Bears off to line his noonday nest.
Not wholly by insidious ease
   Or listless murmurs in the brain
Mastered, I watch the noon increase.
   'Tis something wisely to refrain,
Fling down the mask and keep awhile
   The judgment just, the impulse sane.
Banished the manners that defile,
   The polished lie, the sordid pain,
Banished the venal hand and smile.
   When armies, closing on the plain,
Thunder all day, but at the eve

Give o'er the buffet and the strain
To slumber in a short reprieve,
　While the soft solace of the night
Steeps limbs that bleed and hearts that grieve,
　To some lone watchman on the height
The silence seems surcharged with fate,
　He dreads the hour that brings the light;
Musing what new events await,
　Praying the lawful sword may win,
And ever saying, God is great;
　So, exiled from the smoke and din,
Under the eaves of solitude,
　An eye recluse, unknown to men,
I nurse the meditative mood,
　Divining in my lonely cove
The pulses of the central flood;
　Content with frolic feet to rove,
Drinking the wine, but not the lees,
　A truant heart in vale and grove;
Hearing the harvest-songs of bees,
　The soft nest-chat of dove with dove,
Her voice an olive-branch of peace.

II.

One says, " This fine-fed indolence
   Consumes the bow, displumes the shaft ;
Your arrows miss the deeper sense.
   Come forth to men ; wed hand to haft ;
Reap toilsome sheaves with lawful pain ;
   Find hearth and temple in your craft."
The mystic leaven of the brain,
   The heart divinely turbulent,
The sun-like eye, are these in vain ?
   Few grieve, where all men are content ;
All find, but few are they who seek :
   Too supple creeds, too prone assent !
Grace for the dreamer on the peak,
   Lifting the prayer of asking eyes,
Nor shamed in spirit not to speak
   In plausive scheme or raw surmise,
To chafe his breath to violent wind
   Or patch a ragged world with lies.
Ah ! little blossom of the mind,
   In stillness ray thy purple whorl,

True to the law that shapes thy kind.
    The rains will brim thy bowl with pearl,
The sunbeams kiss thine eyelids red,
    On thee some vagrant bee will furl
His gauzes and from thee be fed ;
    Thy dainty fruit will ripen here,
Thy tender pappus here be shed.

    Not mine to doubt the bond severe,
The weft, the fusion of the Whole,
    A myriad centres, one fair sphere ;
Or that the private spark may roll
    Some beam of virtue through the Vast,
And faintly shape the general goal.
    The fruit of Time, that ripens last,
Will mingle in its juices warm
    Flavors of all the eons past.
Perfect the individual form
    With patient art that works by glee,
Enriched by loss and saved by harm.
    O Life, pervasive, bounteous, free,
I guard the gift thou gavest me,
    The crystal spherule from thy sea.

NOONTIDE.

FALL'N in a deep ambrosial swoon
    The Hóurs, filled full of golden wine,
Slept on the bosom of the noon.
    The passive Sylvans made no sign,
No leaflet fluttered on its roost,
    The rose dreamed sidelong, and the vine
Half-way her drowsy tendrils loosed.
    No feather of breeze; the thistle felt
No airy finger interfused
    Betwixt his silvers : brink-flowers knelt
Brook-wards to cool their lips of fire,
    Lilies perceived their waxes melt.
The bird that wears the bright attire,
    The down of fire-grained Nessean woof,
Burned like a phœnix on her pyre.
    The tortoise quenched his blazing roof
In cool-stemmed grasses, and the bee
    Felt helm and targe, though battle-proof,

Fuse in gold-drippings to his knee.
  Perchance a fledgling zephyr dressed
His tender winglets murmurously,
  Not venturing from his shady nest ;
Or if, hill-born, a bolder breath
  Braved the mid-ether in his quest,
He tumbled in precipitous death,
  Shorn of his frail Icarian fan.
And I, in mossy case beneath
  A leafy lintel, strove to plan
The fancy-bubbles of vague song
  Blown from the gurgling reed of Pan.
But the fine ghosts, an agile throng,
  Slipped through the meshes of my strain,
Elve-syllables, for mortal tongue
  Too wayward.   Then upon my brain
The soft meridional hum
  Beat billowing from the broad champaign,
Over my eyelids poppies clomb,
  And scarce I caught the footfall dumb
Of Slumber through the thicket come.

6

THE THINKERS.

O MERLIN, wise to understand,
   Tiresias, of prevision strong,
Paulus, a bolt from God's right hand,
   Ye fashion, but the world shapes wrong,
Ye lighten, but her paths are dark
   For all your agony, all your song.
The misty gloamings drown your spark,
   Your words are shred on spleenful winds,
Your arrows veer askant the mark.
   She reels in Satyr-rout and binds
Upon her front the dissolute leaf,
   Loves horn and shagg of her brute kinds,
The whirling goat-hoof.   Not for grief
   May ye disroot what ye have sown,
Secure that Fate in his last sheaf
   Will slip some stalks your hands have
      grown,
Will load his shuttle once or twice

With thread of yours for tint or tone.
As gloss that winks on vesper flies,
  Or ghost of Iris none may thrall,
Ye seem in men's bewildered eyes.
  And yet God's elements at your call
Flock, and your trumpets awake the sea
  Old capes to banish, new climes install.
O tangle of sad. humanity,
  Loathed, loved and worshipped in a
      breath,
First knowledge, latest mystery,
  Happy, who through thy forms of death,
Thy barren crusts of winter, spies
  The couchant elf that waits beneath
To flower in amaranthine dyes,
  And lead the vernal sweetness in
With fragrant meadows and flushing skies ;
  Whose ears, though fretted by the din
Of thy vext shoals, where shift and poise
  Folk of fine scale and scarlet fin,
From ocean-margins hears a noise
  Where Freedom from her central deep

Speaks, a still thunder of God's voice;
 Who, pitiful but strong, can keep
A pinion of soft brooding spread
 Above the trouble of thy sleep.
Awake, lift up the sunken head,
 Loosen the shackled tongue and sing,
Grand are the goals to which we tread!
 The leaven of life is leavening,
The type enlarging, strengthening
 From pupa to the perfect wing.

COQUETTE.

O BLITHE new-comer, light-heart breeze,
   Whose frisk and frolic bristle all
The dreamy plumage of the trees,
   Say, can your wanton wit recall,
Since from the beryl-bosomed deep
   You spun your giddy carnival,
The founts at which you paused to steep
   The dewless lip, the boughs whereon
You lodged at night and fell asleep ?
   Under the silver spokes of dawn
Or when the flickering moth shook loose
   Her purfled flounces on the lawn,
Met you, at frolic in the dews
   Or some light wood-lay carolling,
That roving maid who was my Muse ?
   She flies askance, a graceful thing ;

Full of delicious craft and guile,
　　More fitful than a swallow's wing.
It scarce were worth a plain man's while
　　To woo her overmuch, and play
At hazards with her lovely smile,
　　But that at times she bends her way
Unto my threshold, in her eyes
　　Bringing the affluent sun of May :
Ah then she deals in meek replies
　　And lends herself to cheer the house,
With seemly gait, retired and wise ;
　　And, loyal unto household vows,
Plays round the hearth-stone like a beam
　　And takes the honor of a spouse.
Then wear the lawns a festal gleam,
　　The thickets build a marriage-song,
And Undine laughs along her stream ;
　　While high above the gleeful throng
The wood-thrush from his leafy tower
　　Rings, Hymen, Hymen, all day long.
Then feels the rose a golden shower,
　　As when that pair of heavenly line

Held dalliance in the Rhodian bower ;
  With wreaths the cottage-porches shine,
The lintel blossoms, and the flower
  Swarms at the eaves and hangs divine.

THE DRAUGHT.

Bring not the graven cup, I pray,
  Let Hebe forth at her own will;
The wine of gods I slight to-day.
  Beside the spring below the hill
A rusty ladle you may see,
  That half will hold and half will spill.
Let nothing fair the bearer be:
  But pluck the drab from out the street
And let her brim the bowl for me.
  Juice of the earth, I find thee sweet,
Thy salt is honey, soother none,
  And in thy bitter there is meat.
Milk of the rocks, thou lendest tone,
  Iron for blood that feebly runs,
Granite for crumbling arch of bone.
  Who taps not all thy sombre tuns,
O vault of earth, shall never sit
  At revel with Olympus' sons.

So let the abysmal spaces flit ;
 I choose the things of form and bound,
For heavenly sandals, shoes that fit.
 The lordly Dæmons, wisdom-crowned,
Let them in solemn march go by
 Unchallenged on their splendid round ;
Mean things and homely snare my eye,
 Things framed too early, born too late,
And things rejected of the sky.
 For, mindful of her ancient state,
The Soul can still herself adorn ;
 She proudly turns her back on Fate ;
Yea, dares to slight, she, eldest born,
 Pale gods whose race is scarce begun,
And now, for sport, half smiles, half scorn,
 She weaves from shreds and things undone
 A robe so bright it might be spun
 From flaming fleeces of the sun.

METAMORPHOSIS.

BRAKE-FENDED from the brooding gleam,
  The curtains of the eye half-drawn,
I nursed the sultry mid-day dream.
  Lo, clad in garments stained and wan,
Barefooted and unsightly, danced
  A knot of damsels down the lawn,
Plucking, as lightly they advanced,
  Cheap fruit of many a vulgar spray,
Berries or faded flowers, as chanced ;
  Whereof they wove with gestures gay
What seemed a chaplet to my eyes,
  Rude as a child might shape at play.
Though wondering much, I made surmise,
  ' These fashion some fantastic freak,
Elves of the woodland in disguise.'
  With hoods curled backward from the
      cheek,
Dumb lips and paces hush and slow

And something of a reverence meek,
They came and hung about my brow
  The sordid crown, and greeting spake,
But couched in words I did not know.
  Mocked like a dreamer half awake,
I said, ' What seek ye for a game,
  To jeer me for your idlesse' sake ?
Grudge ye the bard his slighted name,
  His hope retired, his simple glee,
The meagre hand's-breadth of his fame ?
  Nathless these weeds are dear to me,
Content from nature's dross to hide
  The leanness of my poverty.'
Too proud for any show of pride,
  I made obeisance to my foes,
Stemming with scorn the craven tide
  That underneath my eyelids rose :
Whereat, as pleased, they smiled and knit
  Their sunburnt palms in circle close
And with shrill songs began to flit
  Round me in wild foot-eddyings,
Like rushing Thyads, fury-smit.

Then slowly, as a day, that springs
Dun from the orient, sweeps aside
The mist that to his forehead clings,
And scales his shining arcs with pride,
Tossing a glance of royal scorn
From zenith to horizon wide,
A purple change o'er these was born ;
Their vesture glowed like clouds that rise
Fresh from the crimson baths of morn.
Wild flickerings vanished from their eyes,
Their feet took measures maidenly,
They sang with burthens mild and wise.
And I beheld that sacred Three,
Who with the Graces walked and him
That framed the lyre in Thessaly ;
The masking Hours, frolic and grim,
And whom they may, deluding sore,
And whom they may not, blessing him ;
The masking Hours, that by our door
In weeds of vagrants daily sit,
And show their seeming trivial store,
Coarse bead or brooch or amulet,

Too mean to buy, too slight to keep ;
And we see not, for all our wit,
The eternal jewels flash and peep,
Immortal prizes, heavenly hoards
Disguised beneath the tinsels cheap.
But while I groped for fitting words
They snapped their rosy links and fled
With laughter like the trill of birds.
I plucked the garland from my head ;
Lo leaf and petal blown anew !
No shrivelled blossoms, but instead
Amaranth, and where the berries grew,
A lucent cyme of stars, and through
The glowing mesh clear beads of dew.

DOOM.

HIGH challenges to valor, heard
 Blown by the trumpet of the wind
Or brought in billet by the bird,
 He, the clear fountain of whose mind
Is curdled by the frog of sense,
 Accepts not, coward all and blind.
His tools of onset and defence
 Moulder ; his hands are lamed and weak ;
The pennon of sweet innocence,
 Unfurled in crimson on his cheek,
Draggles in mire ; his shield of faith
 Half buried lies in odious reek
And caverned by the worms of death :
 The beauteous heraldry of his brow
All tarnished by corroding breath :
 The beams of heaven not struggle through
The turbid liquors of his eye,
 The martial peals he erewhile knew

On the ear's threshold pine and die ;
  His feet are gyved, they will not move,
Languid his limbs of battle lie :
  The crystal phial of his love,
Filled with rank ferments, bursts the heart
  That held it shrined : around, above,
Signals of doom in tempest dart ;
  The temple of his being bows
Upon her bases, breaks apart
  Sundered and wrenched with fateful throes ;
Her lamps are quenched, her portals gride,
  Her altar crumbles where it rose,
Her pillars from beneath her slide,
And through and through her quivering side
The lurid forks of ruin glide.

POETA NASCENS.

WHAT joy to watch the maiden bard
 Trim his Urania's sacred hair
With apple-blossoms and fume of nard ;
 Enchase the sheath with curious care
And gem the hilt of Truth, before
 He girds it on for daily wear ;
Polish a theme in copious store
 Of its own dust, until it shine
A maze of mirrors, a starry core ;
 Daintily card and full his line,
Ingrain with all iridian hues,
 And quilt with passion half divine !
We love him, though his tender Muse
 Touch with rouge-cushioned kitten-paw
The weapons of the world of use.
 We pray his riper rhyme may draw
Some ranging heart to love the yoke
 And take the sober march of law ;

Or yet may cleave with fiery stroke
  Some bond that long has lashed the soul
To Fate's rough Ixionic spoke ;
  Or yet melodiously control
  Blind motions to a fruitful goal
  And fuse them gently in the Whole. .

7

SIGHT-SEEING.

A PURPLE cluster of ripe hours,
 O'erbrimmed with laughter of the sun,
Full of warm winds and irised showers,
 While all the heavens full splendor shone,
From the blue vineyard of the Day
 I plucked and tasted, one by one :
Whose genial wine began to play
 A solstice through the blood, and melt
The frigid thought with mellow ray ;
 And girt my body with a belt
Of eyes, and the diffusive sense
 Stung through its soft nerve-pulps, that felt
Tremors of pleasant violence ;
 Showed me the chosen grots where hide
Coy types and maiden elements ;
 Fleet secrets that forever glide
Meshed in the brook's inseparate twine ;
 Or something of the grace implied

By sunny elve, whose needle fine
   Broiders the peplum of the rose
With tales of love and lore divine ;
   Or on what quest, against what foes
The slashed bee, groping round and round,
   Through flowery Cretan mazes goes,
Unreeling his fine clue of sound ;
   What udders give the humbird suck,
And with what milk their ducts abound ;
   What glebe the robin delves for luck ;
From what uncropped Elysian patch
   The zephyrs myrrh and spices pluck ;
With what brave ethick wood-birds thatch
   The lighter graces of their strain ;
How hollow-out the soul to catch
   The patter of melodious rain
Sprent from the clouds of blossom-fleece,
   Where moulds the thrush her soft refrain ;
How unperplex the characteries
   Etched by the sunbeam in the shade,
Sweet snarl of runic poesies ;
   Or spell the grander scroll displayed

On crumpled hills in pages broad,
　Writ by the quill of Light, arrayed
In all the subtle inks of God ;
　How ravel out the auguries
The pinions of the cloud forebode,
　Or how from mountain-curves to piece
The circle of the universe,
　Or how from Life's own energies
With lawful coin to reimburse
The largess of her affluent purse
And buy a freedom from the curse.

VALOR.

TEMPER the will by day and night
  Flexile as Arab cimeter,
Yet rough as Saxon mace to smite.
  Burnish it fondly : leave no blur :
Pendragon's blade of fate arose
  From mythic depths of character.
Wise Merlin's scrolls perforce disclose
  Their wizard meanings to his eyes ;
He knows by valor what he knows.
  Love draws the sword and saints are wise
To seize a timely bolt of fire
  And storm the gates of Paradise.
Craves the coy goddess of the lyre
  Heroic hands her virgin flower
To pluck, and answer her desire.
  For all fair things are quick with power :
Beauty for mother, strength for sire,
  These gave the world his natal hour.

SONG IN AUTUMN.

THE season of so prosperous birth,
   That came, drew breath and waxed com-
      plete,
Wanes gently, lapsing into dearth.
   Old words are gracious to repeat,
Old songs are welcome to the lyre,
   Old dances pleasant to the feet.
New cycles to the self-same gyre
   Are added ; yet not all the same,
But mixed with hints of something higher.
   Not meanly wise in one poor game,
But on a widening whorl is grooved
   The impulse of the general frame.
Though thought from age to age be moved
   In tedious eddies round the mind
And modern proof be long disproved,
   Not less a simple faith may find,
In forms that upward touch and fuse,

A world-old prescience strong to bind
Fierce contraries to central use;
A flower of Time divinely sprung
From seeds of difference and abuse.
No wanton freak at random flung
To cheer the idlesse of the skies
When gods were wild of blood and young,
And Fate, sleep-heavy in the eyes,
Let slip the distaff for a space;
.But bedded deep in Godhead lies
The method of the starry race,
Filled full of his necessity,
Flushed through with colors of his grace.
Year after year it bides with me
That the supreme sole Form transcends
All type of personality. .
A guess, you say, too far; that lends
Majestic distance to the eye,
But scarce can make the heart amends,
Which craves a nearness, a reply,
A sense of correspondency,
A warmth, a purple in its sky.

THE FIRST SPRING-DAY.

WHILE the raw vales of March were white
    With faded plumules from the vans
Of Winter, as she rose for flight,
    Upon a sunlit crest, by chance,
A threefold group shone in my sight,
    Diverse and strange of countenance:
A shaggy Scythian, fierce in might,
    Snow-drifts along his windy hair,
His eye a dull barbarian light:
    A delicate lady and most fair,
Blue-eyed, a marvellous thing to see,
    Yet something pale of face and spare ;
Holding mid-arm in girlish glee
    A dimpled babe, tender and sleek,
Blanched like a first anemone :
    You spelled the sire on brow and cheek,
But on the lips and in the eyes
    The mother's smile serene and meek.

This baby-blossom of cold skies,
  Born half of winter, half of spring,
Trembles a little where it lies.
  Of it some sweet child-bard should sing,
In whom no flecks of darkness stain
  The silver glosses of his wing.
But I would mingle with my strain,
Darling, too many notes of pain
For days o'erlived in vain, in vain.

THE GOOD MAN.

WOULD'ST taste the sweets of Paradise,
  Walk with the good man in his sphere;
May'st fetch thy Eden from his eyes;
  Whereof the beams are sweet and clear
And holy as the virgin rays,
  Which Morning lays upon the bier
Of Darkness; and within their gaze
  The waste hearts into blossom break,
The dumb lips build a song of praise.
  All safely of his wisdom take,
The signet on whose mouth is peace:
  His simple words are strong to wake
The pure and spiritous melodies
  That cluster round the silent strings
Of the golden harp that hidden lies
  Deep in the heart of each: he flings,
Soft as a zephyr at the eve,
  His spirit o'er it and it rings

Loyally to his suasive hand:

    The imprisoned starry Loves their wings

Open, the solemn Hopes expand;

    The austere majestic Duties wear

Sweet winsome smiles and dimples bland,

    And dance, like holy maids that bear

Rose-garlands, knots of festal hues,

    Round Life and all his common fancs.

His gracious feet can well infuse

    Quick vernal virtues in dead plains,

Kiss the wan cheek of barrenness

    To verdure, and revive its veins,

Whose daily manners have the grace,

    The rigor of the arcs of God,

And in the glory of whose face

    Men read their grandeur; there is showed,

As in a vision, what shall come;

    Large laws unwrit in any code,

The state, the temple and the home

    That wait to make the future plan,

The perfect pillar, the arch, the dome,

    The summits and the goals of man.

O happy threshold he doth tread !
   O happy lintel that doth span
The beauty of his entering head !
   O happy hearth, elect to spread
The cloth, and fetch the good man bread !

APRIL.

WHAT wonder if thy tears and smiles
  Steal from of old the poet's heart,
O fairest queen of sweetest wiles !
  Then let me bring my homely part
Of praise, my violet of rhyme.
  Though nobler bards with better art
Have sung thee many and many a time,
  Bards that could slip into their strain
Some threads of tender or sublime,
  Thou wilt not scorn my weak refrain,
Knowing how sweet a thing it is
  To sing, though all the song be vain.
Cold Nature by thy amorous kiss
  Stung sweetly, stirs his limbs and feels
A thrill of immemorial bliss.
  As a hoar king, whose age congeals

The merry pulse of early years,
   The flush from cheek and forehead steals
And dries the founts of happy tears,—
   Whose servants, seeking through the land,
Have spied among the wheaten ears
   Where maidens reap in comely band,
A creature fashioned wondrously,
   And loosed the sickle from her hand,
And led her in that she may be
   As summer to the wintry king,
As music to his misery,—
   Feeling about his bosom cling
Her glowing arms, and o'er his face
   Her flowery breath flow murmuring,
Loving her for her delicate grace,
   Her tender palm of blandishment,
Her gracious eyes and winsome ways,
   Perceives his frosty thews relent,
A subtle blossom in his blood,
   Soft throes of passionate intent ;
So quickens up to leaf and bud
   The frore earth in thy fervent arms

And gets his youth in fiery flood.
   Now, while the brook forgets his harms,
The meadows hatch the flowery brood,
   The breeze runs riot with thy charms,
Bring to the bard his proper good,
   Season, to him who loves thee well;
And melting down his colder mood,
   Teach all the tender buds to swell,
The buds of song; pansy, primrose
   And crocus, these that know thy spell.
And each young blossom as it blows
   Shall breathe thy love, thy glory tell,
At morn and when its petals close.

II.

Now all fair natures out of night
   Break, and put on their strength and thrive,
Blending their essence with the light.
   The pulseless masses heave and strive,
Rude silence flowers to sweetest song,
   And saddest creatures woo and wive.

With harp and lute, in choric throng,
   The first-born children of the year,
In virgin weeds, untouched by wrong,
   On sunny levels make their cheer,
Pitching bright tents of brief sojourn.

   Thanks, darlings, for the omen dear,
The message of your blithe return ;
   That all the firm old centres hold,
And all regard the self-same bourn :
   Large space for action, as of old,
For eye to seek, for light to shine,
   And meeds and glories manifold.
O season, give me of thy wine :
   I rend the sombre suit of grief
And make a seemly gladness mine ;
   That while the world in transport brief
Bursts into jets of curious flame
   And slowly builds the perfect leaf,
I lie not cramped by sullen shame,
   But sandalled with an emulous fire,
Be parcel of the splendid game.
   All things forevermore aspire :

Nor can I slacken or make pause

This side the goal of pure desire.

Then give me of thy wine that thaws

Hopes and delights too long frost-bound

Under the might of ruder laws.

O thyrsus-laden, chaplet-crowned

Young Mænad of a rite sublime,

Lift up a dithyrambic sound ;

Evoe ! while the ambrosial prime

Beats in all veins a living rhyme

And generous madness pure of crime.

8

MY HOUSE.

THE pillars of my house are strong,
   God gives Himself for fundament,
The beams of Fate to her belong.
   Though fugitive as Arab tent,
Elusive as a Libyan mist,
   Where frailest, most a firmament.
Ply mine or petard, as ye list,
   Flood with red flame her chambers all,
Bring Jötun, Titan to assist,
   Ye win no feeblest prop to fall,
Nor scathe the poorest tint that dyes
   The sheen of her translucent wall.
Lo, many men in anger rise,
   The peoples trample, and the zones,
Stung with infuriate energies,
   Clamor with broil of hostile thrones ;
A thousand interests, whelmed in gore,
   Sink, and the wounded planet moans.

She keeps unshaken, as before,
   Her solemn proud serenity,
And on the plinth before her door
   Sits Peace ; beside her, Harmony.
Wherefore in her mẏ heart will wear
   Triumphal vests of faith and glee.
For musing on her type with care,
   A crystal without flaw or seam,
All inly stablished and most fair,
   Feeling from architrave and beam
A silent grandeur fall to bless,
   From shaft and dome a gladness stream,
I cry, ' It is a goodly grace
   A little while the courts to tread,
A little while, of this sweet place,
   Until the weanling soul be bred
To universal qualities ;
   Until Time wither and be shed
Like petals from the fruiting trees,
And Sense, a snow-flake, thaw and cease,
And life to life be power and peace.'

FREEDOM.

O THOU, who dwellest with the wise,
   Bride of the spirit, flower of light,
Mother of all fair energies,
   Not my weak sonnet may recite,
Freedom, thy strong fair sanctity,
   Or paint thy glorious walk aright.
Yet oft on twilight hills I see
   Thy form august, and feel thy power
And speak, as friend with friend, with thee.
   So must the fond muse hour by hour
Hover and hum about thy sweet,
   Or skirt the fringes of thy bower.
In impious times it scarce is meet
   To sound thy holier rites, or bare
Thy threshold to unwashen feet;
   For they that should have found thee fair
Misprize thee; yea, thy children turn
   Their hands to rend thee and not spare.

As those dear limbs, that knew no urn,
  Bruised, gashed, forlorn, strewn far and
    near
For suns to blacken, tides to spurn,
  For which young Isis many a year
Goaded her fleet papyrean prow,
  And blistered Nilus with her tear,
Thou liest diffused, dishevelled, thou
  Dismembered ; loosed thy golden knots,
The grandeur filched from off thy brow.
  Thy lovers seek thee in strange spots
And find about thy sacred shards.
  The tender dear forget-me-nots.
Lo, these thy warriors, these thy bards,
  Faithful, will gather thee complete,
Cleanse thee in spices and pure nards,
  Close all the cruel seams, reknit
The ravelled thews, and all the broad
  Proportions model and refit ;
Till thou, relumed with life from God,
  With thunder clad, with lightning shod,
  Break all thy foes beneath thy rod.

A PYTHONESS.

RUDE Pythia of my mossy grotto,
   Lank blossom, prithee, breathe for greet-
      ing
Some Golden Verse, some Delphic Motto.
   Beggar and lone I come entreating,
Knowing thine almsdeed without malice,
   Thine alms not minished for repeating.
I pine in my resplendent palace
   Built of world's wit, prescripts of sages;
I thirst beside the poet's chalice,
   Am sadder for the master's pages,
And ever count my treasure leaner
   For testaments of all the ages.
My wealthiest having shows far meaner
   Than this vast want for aye increasing,
Wise answers bring me pangs far keener
   Than questions that will find no easing :
Worship not stoops to our devotion,

Beauty wings lightly past our seizing.
Like mariner athirst from ocean,
I sought these dewy haunts, beseeching
Some well-spring, some miraculous potion.
But Fate, my foolish thought outreaching,
Part for a mockery, part for warning,
Left his evangel for thy preaching.
My bold sweet Cynic, coldly scorning
In worsted poverty the gleaming
Sidonian tints thy mates adorning,
I something glean from thy plain seeming
To chide my humor.   Yet another
And deeper lore is round thee beaming :
'Twas this I came for, this, no other ;
The lore of Love, all lores revoking,
Of Love, the wisest, mightiest mother.
Though wit should fail, heart's strength be
        broken,
O Soul, let her high name be spoken,
Her light be an eternal token.

A FURLONG from the hearth of man,
 Blown from the frontlet of a hill,
Murmured the evening voice of Pan :
 "All day my lips with breathings thrill
The sacred sevenfold Nomian reed,
 All day with drifts of music fill
The soft hill-fold and billowy mead,
 But none comes forth equipped to hear,
The song to fathom, the myth to read.
 My embassies of love and cheer
Are thrust with hoot and buffet forth
 The rabbled gateway of man's ear.
And ye, whose lips by power of birth
 Sing ope the wards of Fate and heir
The ancient fulness of the earth,
 Bards, born of the azure, tell me where
Lies bound the daring muse that brought
 Her songs from high above the air ?

Ye slacken : lo, ye wane to nought.
 Your silken idlesse coos and purrs,
Unquarried lies the toilsome thought.
 I feel about my steadfast spurs
The chime and patter of your feet,
 That chase my shredded gossamers.
Ye chirr and chirrup, buzz and bleat,
 Ye glass yourselves in bubbles fine,
Or, beardless Satyrs, round my seat
 Reel from the foam-pink of my wine,
Or ravel a sunbeam for trope
 To gild the leanness of a line.
Soft hands of dalliance break not ope
 My thrice-barred ninefold mystery,
Smooth vowel-liquid rhymes not cope
 With the height and depth of melody.
Praise to my lordly sons that sleep !
 O immemorial phantasy,
Whose boreal pencils lit the steep
 And flushed the utmost brow of heaven !
Fire-breathing hill, world-girding deep
 For playthings to thy hands were given,

And down thy broad creations streamed
  Opulent tints of morn and even.
What brave delight of old it seemed,
  When all the Arcadian flock-sown lawns
With Time's auroral warblings teemed !
    The pine-brakes frolicked, changed to
        fawns,
Yea, every shepherd blew his oat
  In light of crimson-glimmering dawns.
While browsed or whisked the wanton goat,
  I felt them clamber round my knees,
Ravished and rapt upon my note :
  With souls like lips of thirsting bees,
They clung and sucked my honeyed stops,
  Until their melody-drunken glees
Made pant the multitudinous copse
  And dance the silver-footed springs,
The mountain tingle to his tops.
  But ye—ye fondle barren strings,
Too dull for any strain of mine,
  Too feeble ; which the man who sings
Maddens his numbers with a wine,

Whose grape ne'er purpled hill or plain,
Dæmoniac, kinsman to divine."
  Listening, with heavy shame and pain
Stricken, I staggered and fell prone,
  And broken-hearted was full fain
To blend with silence and have done,
Since more forlorn my lyre is grown
Than hollow bone that clanks on bone.

OPEN HOUSE.

HOLD open house; dwell not apart:
　Spread forth a liberal board, and keep
A world-wide welcome in the heart.
　To entertain the gods is cheap:
They come in dusty rags, and crave
　A little bread, a little sleep.
Make haste, arise, give all you have;
　The beggar's staff to Mercury's rod
Will change, the wrinkles of the knave
　To the bright features of a god,
And into wings of fire the shoes
　With which his homely feet are shod.
Borne upon every wind, the Muse
　Beats at the casements of the bard
With freightage of melodious news:
　But all is dark; he keepeth guard;
She cannot find a chink or rent:
　To bless the overwise is hard.

The pallid prisoner, worn and bent,
  Through scrolls of magic peeps and pores,
Handling with a sublime intent
  Forgotten spells : lo, at his doors
The spirit-feet of Ariel wait
  Whom he laboriously implores.
Fling wide, O fool, the grate, the gate,
  The couriers knock, the dæmons throng,
Accept, accept the bounteous fate.

  Nay, rather let me suffer wrong
Than slight the meanest elve that brings
  The symbol and the soul of Song.
Bear hence the mighty harp that flings
The epic thunder from its strings,
For I will chant rejected things.

REMINISCENCE.

I.

Too much of Lethe: I would fain
  Relume the faded types that lie
Dark in the mazes of the brain.
  I have forgot my native sky,
The cot where I was born of old,
  The beauteous forms that passed thereby ;
Forgot the happy lawns I strolled,
  The flowers that thronged about my door,
Ambrosial purple, immortal gold ;
  Forgot the beach I frolicked o'er,
  The ocean, whose smaragdine floor
  Reposed unswept by mortal oar.

II.

Could I but frame a knot would hold
  Thy slippery spirit for a span,

O thou, through whom the cheerless wold
    Takes on a feature and a plan,
By whom it winks and smirks and sues
    And has the smiles and voice of man;
Could I but stay thee in a noose,
    Shy brook, I would not let thee free
Till thou hadst answered for the muse
    With whom I travail; showed to me
In what coy cove or mossy glen
    Is hid thy fount of Memory;
That drinking, I might hear again
    Feet of the first-born Periods,
That long before the birth of men,
    Shod with the buskins of the gods,
Sported upon the ethereal mead;
    Might hear the strong creative odes
Gush from the Amphionian reed
    Of the joyous overflowing Fate,
And see the rosy Eon lead
    To the blithe dance her blushing mate,
Nature, apparelled as a bride,
    Opening soft her maiden gait,

With lilies garlanded, the pride
   Of heavenly gardens ; ah ! might see
The choric motion billowing wide,
   Like foam-fringed circles on the sea,
Divinely maddened ;—to the measure,
   From crypts of deep eternity,
To join the eddying deepening pleasure
   Steal elemental forms and features,
Atomic throngs, a goodly treasure,
   And all the balanced lordly creatures,
And arm in arm and foot to foot
   Wheeling, they blend their diverse nat-
      ures ;
Or, changed into a beam, might shoot
   And kiss the everlasting hills
When all things holy hang as fruit,
   And the sole Essence stirs and thrills
The luminous boughs, a whispering breeze,
   Or a fine perfume, folds and fills
The sleeping valleys : till with ease
   I clear at one heroic bound
The pale of Time, and proudly cease
   From the Day's inharmonious round,

Yea, on the breast of that which is

    Melt like a flake of softest sound.

Dost mock so steep a hope as this,

    Wise Brook, and bid me go my way

Too fragile for such weight of bliss ?

    Alas, thy ripples frown and say,

" This rapture crowns not every spirit,

    And not all men remember may.

Dear is a song, for you can hear it,

    And sweet a rose, for you can scent it,

But God's ripe splendor, who can bear it ?

    Who drinks my fountain may repent it.

Such fiery ferments and so rare

    The long eternal suns have lent it.

And Temperance guards with falchion bare

    This stately wassail of the heart,

And sifts all men that enter there.

    To know the grandeur of this art,

One must be white as washen wool,

    Austere and whole in every part.

And yet 'tis from of old the rule,

    These hostile poles should inter-dart

As warp and woof the poet's soul."

A MOOD.

BE mine to-day the pastoral crook,
　For flock, the floweret's tufts of fleece,
For food, the simples by the brook.
　Fold up the ponderous mysteries :
Chance-wafted gossamers of thought
　I pluck from ringlets of the breeze.
Great Pan himself will not be caught ;
　Enough to hear from whispering rush
The soul of Syrinx faintly brought,
　To find a fillet on the bush
Fresh-fall'n from Sinoë's shaken hair.
　Although not mine the waves that gush
From uplands of Parnassian air,
　Where the Camœnæ proudly sing
Of what is Lawful, what is Fair,
　Let me, at leisure wandering,
Just when the morning opens, pass
　That sweetest Acidalian spring,

And spy upon the flowery grass

    Aglaia's winsome footprint shine.

Yea if, in brimming oft the glass,

    I falter from the perfect nine,

    Rather than fail of things divine,

    The lesser lovelier three be mine.

THREE COUNSELLORS.

HER cloak of Twilight fluttering wide,
  Saddled upon a ridge of wind,
The Eve slid crone-wise to my side.
  With beaked and shadowy palm she
    signed ;
She pulled her hood about her eyes
  And doled me alms of her dark mind.
" Flee not, but listen and be wise :
  Go strip the laughter from thy heart
And wear for girdle thorns and sighs.
  Grain in thy flesh with studious art,
For woad, despair ; nay, sting thy soul
  With death and hell for wholesome smart.
Embrace my gloom : assume my cowl :
  From my Tartarean wells of fire
Mantle thy muse's myrrhine bowl.
  Bristle thy verse with rough desire :
Is it so soft a thing to sing ?

Sad be the man that holds the lyre :
He bears the whole world on his string,
   To it is bound a struggling god,
And utmost Fate folds there her wing.
   Then wed thee to my ancient blood :
Get thee for chords strong agonies
   And in flame-sheets of tempest flood
Thy soul across them ; moult thy case
   And wipe the honey from thy lip ;
Thy words shall shame and shock, not
      please."
   Anon on heaven's eastern steep
Night's weary guards sank prone among
   Their pining picket-fires asleep.
And through the cloud-camp loosely flung,
   I saw the opal arrows play,
Of Morning, as he strolled along.
   A rosy flake of orient spray
He shattered on my lids and smiled,
   And sweetly gesturing seemed to say,
" What lip has stricken thee, poor child ?
   What gnome waylaid thy wonted glee,

Damped all thy valor, thy wit beguiled ?
　Rise, mix thy yearning heart with me :
Fledge with my aimless breeze thy heel,
　Put on my purples and with me flee.
Who heirs from heaven the lyre, should feel
　Motions of mighty mirth within :
Hades he tames ; can sinless steal
　His will from the Amathusian queen ;
The forks of Jove are quenched in song,
　And the soothed Sisters kindlier spin.
The lyre is sword and armor strong,
　The lyre is patience, peace and power,
Only the lyre can do no wrong.
　Stale not thy heart with sighs, nor sour
With musty wit, but for thy strain
　Speed lightly to Thalia's bower.
Nor stay thy numbers to explain,
　But bolt the toilsome muse at home,
And slight with me thy studious pain.
　Bright hints and graceful plans will come
From ripple of grass and throat of dove,
　The hills be tabrets where you roam,

And every rill Castalia prove,

    Love-strophes round all blossoms play,

Dodona speak from every grove."

    I mused which parlance to obey :

" Both," spake the broad serene Midday,

    " Knead matin red with vesper gray."

A MORNING ENCOUNTER.

DEAR bird, whose song slid on a beam
    From some watch-turret of the dawn
Betwixt my sleep and broke my dream,
    Calling me, while the east was wan,
To hear thy voluble oracle
    Pronounced with pomp to grove and lawn,
Would I might shape my rhyme to tell
    The giant measure of my debt
For that great fortune which befell.

    For while through meads my course was
        set,
Washed with the foam of new-made light
    And purple-veined with violet,
I saw upon an orient height
    A child-like shape, yet ripe as man,
The color of his vesture white.
    He beckoned me : and I began
To think some spirit of the Blue

Had shortened here his lucid van.
Too glorious, to my troubled view,
  For any creature of the womb,
The temper of his body grew
  Transpicuous as a censer's fume,
Or weft of iris on the plain,
  Or, virgin from an antique loom,
Sendal or samite without stain,
  Till all his essence was made bare,
Pure and undimmed by mortal pain,
  Milk-white and perfect, without scar;
And over all, meseemed, was spread
  The splendor of the morning-star.
Long while he searched my eyes, then said,
  " Brother, the fulgent runes of God
May best in such an hour be read,
  While mightiest instincts are abroad,
The ether quick with holy spells,
  The gnomes of darkness overawed ;
While fine dæmoniac syllables
  Are busy round the couchant ear,
And Fate's eternal canticles

Sound o'er us, easy now to hear,
And on the crowning branch of Thought
  The spirit perches without fear.
Now all that ever we have sought
  Is proffered : let our hearts be knit
Serenely."   As an eagle fraught
  With all his youth, when vapors flit
That masked the sun, puts on his might
  To sail into the blaze of it,
His fancy steered in venturous flight
  Wings of no mortal plumage wove,
Through radiance that made blank the sight,
  Straight to the tale that seraphs love ;
How in the old abysmal gloom
  A plastic breath was taught to move,
And then a luminous flower to bloom,
  The effluence of whose petals strove
The dark circumference to illume ;
  Its mystic fragrance, which was Love,
Rose through the deeps in melody ;
  From whorl to beaming whorl it throve,
A form of wondrous symmetry,

Delighting the waste fields of air,
The darling of Eternity;
    And how its pollen burst in fair
Broad flakes of stars, and every one
    Took of God's beauty, each his share,
And fired with duteous motions, spun
    Harmonious.   When his utterance ran
Through all the meaner grades and won
    The sacred blossoming of Man,
The imperial theme wrought in his song
    Such height as only spirits can.
What beams unto his orb belong
    He traced in fire, and all his proud
Forecastings, and his power of wrong;
    Broke through the sensuous mists that
        shroud,
And drew with high and solemn glee
    His spirit naked from the cloud,
Shorn of all lesser faculty,
    And elemented of white flame,
And matchless for its unity;
    And urging still his soaring aim,

Borne upon numbers wild and free,
  With sound of many a secret name
And the large sense of poesy
  And wisdom drawn from either pole,
In stately sequence loftily
  He sang the triumphs of the Soul,
And with what subtile links is bound
  Its being to the perfect Whole.
And when he closed, the fields around
  Trembled in waves of light, and flowers
Burgeoned in fire from underground,
  And buds from all the rosy bowers
Of the great Dawn broke and fell fast
  Against my face in dazzling showers,
And visions rapt me, and I cast
  My body upon earth and slept,
Captive to dreams of purport vast;
  Till the sun came and sunbeams crept
About their favorite sense, and pried
  My lids asunder: and I wept
To find no dæmon by my side,
  But only birds that sang of him,

Till looking westward I espied
    Upon the champaign's purple rim
The lustre of his raiment shine,
    And caught a smile, though far and dim,
And something no man may define,
A gesture, a celestial sign
That this fair creature was divine.

EVENING SONG.

THE fragrant hollows of the air
  Murmur with interfluent power,
And all is poesy or prayer.
  And summoned by the affluent hour,
The soul with paces of delight
  Steals like a maiden from her bower
To meet her lover : dæmons bright
  Flit in and out the silver doors
And haunt the porches of the night :
  And friendly signals from far shores
Beacon, and the rich heaven streams
  With love through all its shining pores.
Truths, wont to glance in fickle gleams
  Across the shadowy gulf of things,
Burn out like stars, their burnished beams
  Summed and full-sheaved : Eolian strings
Sound in the poet's breast, his heart
  Leaps like a roe, and all the springs

Of being into fulness start :
　He feels the tightening of the bond
That links his own with Nature's heart.
　He thrills, he waves his mystic wand,
And songs, from bosoms of the wind
　Flocking, unto his lure respond :
Like moths they flutter round his mind,
　Manifold shapes, a hundred hues
Glimmering : he is too gay to bind
　Their fleet-foot revels; and his muse
Laughs inly at her great opulence.
　He feels the earth's firm fabric fuse,
And all the frozen forms of sense
　Thaw into plastic waves, and Time
Bow to some vaster influence.
　Yea Nature, like a ghostly mime,
Moults her gross mask and slips away,
　Her seeming discords change to rhyme,
Her steadfast bases will not stay,
And all her ponderous timbers weigh
Light on the soul as beams of day.

A CHARACTER.

FORLORN, who chantest hollow dirge,
   From under damp Trophonian caves,
Of primal lapse and final scourge,
   Lauding the life that deepest grieves,
The brow that girds itself with night,
   The hope that chills us and bereaves;
Whose tongue with subtle and sweet delight
   Tastes, eloquent, the soul's disgrace
And laps the garbage of her plight;
   Whose pencil paints her glorious face
Defaced, her breasts deflowered and rent,
   Her azure eyes opaque and base;
Carving thy meagre lineament
   Upon her mountains of vast woe;
Making her shame thy ornament,
   To lend thy thunders pitch and glow,
Thy dead evangels nerve and hue;

Even thee I hate not, since I know
There's little wholly false or true :
Yet thanked be Zeus, who erewhile knew
To frame a planet would hold two.

10

SOOTHSAYERS.

O HONEY-SWEET in thought and voice,
    Soothsayers washed in odorous dews,
On whom the peoples fix their choice,
    What tidings from the Heavenly Muse,
What fair prescript of law and light,
    Purged of the taint of modern use ?
Ah perfumēd martyrs for the right,
    Rare watchmen, coming in at even,
Bold warriors, virgin of the fight !
    So gently amorous of heaven,
So coy of haste and zealous fire,
    Your lapses hardly count to seven.
Profane ! Not scrupling to desire
    The awful pearls of God to aid
The dazzle of your cheap attire.
    Have ye seen Beauty ? Has she laid
A weight of splendor on the brain,
    Till all the man was sore afraid ?

Ye ply much suppliance in vain :
 Who wins her perfect smiles, must bring
A greatness of another strain :
 For though her face is bland as spring,
Oh gentlier-eyed than any flower
 Divinest in its blossoming,
Yet on her forehead hour by hour
 Lighten like stars of Araby
The solemn symbols of her power ;
 Crown over crown in majesty,
A brightness builded like a tower,
 A million lights in harmony.

LAW.

WHAT knightly port of man draws near,
  What hero carved from the antique,
What child of battle and the spear ?
  Full-armed he rides by lawn and creek,
Fenced, breast and thigh, in glorious scale,
  The visor dark on brow and cheek.
O creature fashioned to prevail,
  What errand, what ideal quest,
What sainted shrine, what holy grael ?
  Ever his lance is poised in rest,
Ever his glances search afield,
  Ever before his pillared breast
The fulgent orbit of his shield
  Makes splendor, like a captive sun ;
And on it, graved in ample field,
  The letters of his motto run,
"The perfect Law." O dauntless heart!
  Proud goal forever never won !

Behold from brake and glen they start,
　All shapes that bear the name of foe;
Whatever pierces with the dart,
　Whatever bends afar the bow;
And monsters of the middle air
　Wheel o'er his march in circle slow,
Or sweep on thunder-plumes to tear.
　But nothing prospers to his harm:
Midway they pause, stung with despair.
　For something fateful in his arm,
Something of terror on his plume
　Melts with the breath of mad alarm
Their order, and completes their doom:
　Like mist they drift in wracks of flight,
Swift blasts confound, strange fires consume.
　Mayhap he stirs himself for fight
To wipe some dark plague from the earth;
　Who sees him strike, would guess the
　　　might
Of every god in heaven went forth.
　His broadening purpose knows no bar:
A sleepless warrior from his birth,

From bourn to sliding bourn afar
He rides, of lawless enmity
   The mock and mark by sun or star.
He, without sorrow, without glee,
   And mingling not with love or hate,
Knows one strong word, Necessity.
   Sure hands of a conclusive Fate
Work out to men through sword and lance,
   Through what they shatter, what create.
Not short nor over nor askance
   The pith of his endeavor falls :
No slip, no halt ; his steps advance
   Through what seduces, what appalls ;
Clear in the counsel of his mind,
   He works his will, whate'er befalls.
Him yield full praise : ye will not find
'   His equal by the land or sea,
And yet a greater than his kind,
   It is my dream, will come to me,
   Larger in bearing and degree,
   And of diviner race than he.

LOVE.

THE best among the sons of men,
 God led up hither for a grace :
Such luck, I guess, comes not again.

 Unknown his name, for our two ways
Had never crossed since time began,
 Our eyes not mixed their kindred rays.
Yet had I spoken with this man
 Ere the blue firmament was spun,
Or the first star his circuit ran.

 No casque nor cuirass on him shone,
Nor guise of any martial thing ;
 His foe breathed not beneath the sun.
All natures gave him welcoming,
 Yea, warring kings ungirt their ire
To fetch him a love-offering.

 The omens writ in signs of fire,
The thunders of an angry law,
 The startings of half-crushed desire

Raged far below him : for he saw
   Beyond the knitted brows of night,
Where meaner spirits fail for awe,
   That ocean of serenest light ;
So was he gladdened as a child
   That gambols in its mother's sight.
The sweetness of his mien beguiled
   All things to yield him of their best :
From hideous forms, from brute and wild
   He drew by charms the holiest,
The fairest. Fate's most rude intent
   Fell like a rose upon his breast.
Ah ! unto him the gods had lent
   Power so sure, repose so even,
He never sighed nor toiled nor bent.
   Albeit all he asked was given,
No sign he made, he shaped no vow,
   Nor seemed at all to crave of Heaven.
But as the plume above the brow
   Of some divinely tempered knight
Cheerily dances whether he go
   To mix with pastime or with fight,

His deed, that stayed a lapsing race
   And sowed the dreary wastes with light,
Seemed a slight symbol of his grace,
   Hovered above him airily,
And could not flatter from his face
   The lofty dear simplicity :
Yet all his speech was tuned thereby
   Unto a deeper melody,
And all the glances of his eye
   Lined with a finer majesty.
Once more, yet once before I die,
   Ye gracious years, lead him to me
Or me to him, that Life may know
   The grandeur of her ministry ;
Till her frore fountains break and flow
Down from these polar crests of snow
To the warm Eden spread below.

A DREAM.

WHILE the night-flower, Sleep, inbreathed
   Her perfume deepest in the brain
And softly soul and sense inwreathed
   With dreams, her blossoms, one of grain
More delicate and richer dye
   I culled, therewith to trim my strain.
To the tranced fantasy of my eye,
   Three luminous lilies tall and white,
In a Hesperian plot of sky
   Burgeoned from amber beds of light,
And waxed full petal and throve a space,
   Till a weird breath of subtle blight
Fell on them and licked out their grace.
   Thereon a threefold fruit they bore,
That splitting spouted jets of rays
   And changed to mighty orbs that wore
Marvels of brilliance : one like Jove,
   When his large brows are lavished o'er

With temperate beams ; like her, one throve,
    Who in soft internebular mead
At dayfall fastens dove to dove,
    Bruising with yoke their purple brede ;
The third a tremulous opal, pale
    And red, that ran with rhythmic speed
Through all the notes of Iris' scale.
    Anon my dream slid down to earth,
Where frolicked in brook-garrulous vale
    Three children that pursued with mirth
Quick wink of night-fly or what thing
    Their light moods graced with passing worth.
But when those Splendors, beckoning,
    Lured their wild eyes, they straight forsook
The idlesse of their travailing.
    Soul-buoyed in strong ecstatic look,
Breathless stood each, as saint who sees
    God's finger writing in a book.
And from them shot with sudden ease
    Wings woven of empyreal fire,
That, stung with starry memories,
    Yearned, thrilled and flickered with desire

To taste their lawful element.

    Then quivered, like a fervid lyre

At Phœbus' tender blandishment,

    Those spirits with instinctive throes,

And from their mortal prisonment

    Timorous and faintly fluttering rose ;

Like moths, that through the fissured floss

    Bursting, their silver films disclose.

But when their bolder steerings cross

    The circle where the vapors cruise,

Fierce flaps of tempest, jarring, toss

    Their oarage in wild pools, and bruise

Their feathery lacings, and their glow

    O'ertarnish with malicious dews.

Anon the gulf of air below

    Broke into showers of colored flame ;

False lights meteorous to and fro

    The dusk abysm went and came

In mad corant and glittering maze,

    Lewd motions shadowing feats of shame.

Each spangle in the whirling chase

    Began to pant voluptuously,

Dilated, changed, and took the phase
  . Of nymph or maiden marvellously :
A passionate bosom here, whereon
  Lily and rose were fair to see ;
There becked an amorous arm ; and one
  Pouted lush lips in act to kiss ;
One throbbed like Venus' mystic zone.
  Here laughed that treacherous queen of
      bliss
Who turned her suitors out to graze,
  With tusks to grunt, with coils to hiss ;
There she, the sharp sword of whose face
  Smote host and counter-host and slew,
And hacked gray Ilion to his base.
  And while those daring children flew
Baffled and vapor-clogged and lame
  In slackening gyres, half lost to view,
One, hopeless of the arduous game,
  Seduced by that coruscant glare,
Forgot his ardors and heart-tame
  Swerved down : whereon a dying flare
Shot from his wings, that blackening rolled

Two drifts of smoke, and everywhere
Wide dragon-gorge and serpent-fold
  Writhed, yawned ; and things of bristling
      hide
Their bestial tongues with famine lolled.
  These gulphed him headlong : and I sighed,
Yea well-nigh waked for moan and pain
  At him who marred his virgin pride.
Then rose from mountain-ridge and plain
  Innumerable clamors rude,
A hoarse malign derisive strain.
  And I beheld a multitude
Swarm like a locust-cloud, whose rain
  Leaves all a fruited champaign nude.
These could not their false hearts refrain
  At quenching of that creature bright,
But roared a tempest of disdain.
  The hardier twins in dauntless flight
Clove the dark belt of mist, and glode
  High through the tideless waves of light.
But one drooped, faltering from his road ;
  Less studious of the opulent skies

And those three glorious goals of God,
   Than of the herd whose voices rise
Thridding the labyrinths of his ear
   Soft as the feet of melodies.
By them he tacks his voyage, veers
   To match their humors ; who reply,
Battering the concave with brute cheers.

   O wonder ! from brow, breast, and thigh
Three emerald wisps sprang, such as lure
   To midnight ooze the traveller's eye.
These, wheeled in many a fickle tour,
   Waylaid him and confused his thought,
Till he forgot those splendors pure,

   And reached a maddened hand and caught
Their hollow-glimmering essences
   And in his hair their lustres wrought ;
Now changed to forky tongues, a tress
   Of green ophidian twine, that freeze
His brain with lithe and cold caress.

   Whereon his plumes by quick degrees
Sicken and pale, their perfect type
   Shrivelled in sad and dark decrease.

And he, his giant error ripe,
   Plumped sheer amidst the seething throng,
That shrieked, smote tymbal and blew pipe,
   And thundering many a sordid song
Haled him triumphal, couched on gold,
   Through reek of praise and bellowings
     strong.
But when this noisome clangor rolled
   Past touch of sense, I laughed for glee
To mark that holier spirit hold
   His heavenly quest in circles free,
Swathed in such sheets of radiance
   The vision wrestled e'en to see
His plumage winnowing. But his vans,
   Meseemed, flushed with impassionate hues
And strengthened. Then in deeper trance
   I saw those sovereign splendors loose
Three awful hands from forth the blaze,
   And in each palm for spiritous use
A pencil of immortal rays,
   Which he ensheathed deep in his soul.
No more I witnessed, such the daze

That whelmed me.　But from pole to pole
A pulse of gladness seemed to run,
　A tremor of melody through the Whole.
Unto a hidden grove, to shun
　Men's eyes, this spirit paced alone,
　And no man wist what he had done.
　　11

OMENS.

I.

WHAT cheerful omens flush the skies
 For those that watch the years' slow birth
With doubtful hearts and sober eyes ?
  " A low hard wailing from the earth !
A flood, world-wide, without an ark !
 A time of blackness and of dearth ! "
Is all so sad ? Is Hope made dark
 On all her altars, and no priest
Awake to feed the fainting spark ?
  " The devils flocking to the feast,
The lie enshrined, the bating trust,
 Signs of the sceptre of the Beast ;
The clash of bruits, the surge of dust,
 And chaos, whetted claw and beak,
With feverous eyes of burning lust
 Hovering like night above the reek ;

Wisdom, an eyeless Cyclops, strong
   To waste the thing he would but seek ;
Fair Youth, that lopped the boughs of
      wrong,
   Planting the same in hoary age,
And bards grown careless of the song,
   And saints with prayers that turn to rage ;
Fierce humors, which the poisonous broth
   Of discord only can assuage ;
These and a thousand ills, the froth
   Of life and fate, are plain to see,
While good men falter or wax wroth,
   Toiling with sad hard energy
To cleanse the surface of the pool,
   Leaving the fetid oozes free."
What then ?   Shall ancient ardors cool,
   And madness, all unthwarted, base
Secure the bulwarks of his rule ?
   Thank God, not yet ; while one sure place
Abides to stay the planted foot,
   There fight the battle of the race.
More fire will yield us less of soot.

Breathe deeper ; summon power from far,
Nor crave a rash and sudden fruit.

Nay, let no coward lesson mar
The creed of hope, the brave man's creed,

Summit and sum of what we are.
Welcome, whose eyes are wise to read

What gracious auguries are born
From prophet's word or hero's deed.

If many monstrous things forlorn,
In lawful silence wrapt, are laid

Deep out of sight, too poor for scorn ;
If many hearts of youth are swayed

By thoughts that nurse a richer hour
Than those for which their fathers prayed ;

If Reverence shape a fairer flower,
And the great Soul be prescient

Within herself of purer power,
Trust, while the patient bright Event

Through rifts across her ancient shell
Thrusts pinions of divine intent.

Too faithless ! meanly thus to tell
The beads of hope.　Though demon hands

Flung gaping every door of hell,
And men relapsed to broken bands,
  One heart will not his faith deny
While one cool morn her flower expands,
  Or through the darkling wrack on high
  One cheerful fleck of azure sky
  Smiles courage to the drooping eye.

II.

For while a miasm in the blood
  Freezes and fires a fickle race,
Fate-harried, ignorant of the Good,
  Some tokens of immortal grace
Visit the spirit large in trust,
  Who, seated in her inmost place,
Across the gurge of foolish dust,
  Reads on the sky in fiery trace
The final triumph of the just.

III.

O Freedom ! theme caressed by all,
  The loudest voiced, least understood,

It little profits to recall
  Thy solemn traits and holy mood,
Or of the bond severe to tell,
    That makes thee one with Truth and
      Good.
Yet thou alone canst breathe the spell
  That works within the soul of man
The wise and perfect miracle.
    His powers long mouldering under ban
'Tis thine to rescue, and give back
  Their crowns and sovereignty again ;
Till, 'scaping from the slime and wrack,
    Re-poised on her aërial,van,
The spirit mounts her starry track,
  Nor fears to prove the antique plan,
When through the tempest and the fire
  Man talked with God and He with man.
Arise, O Man, from-dust and mire,
  Regather in a lordly hour
Thy stature and thy proud desire.
    Build with sweet patience and sure power
Thy greatness up through arch and dome,

Thy strength through citadel and tower.
No more in shameful exile roam :
Taught of thy birth and lineage,
Be to thyself a heaven and home.

Write down a fresh historic page ;
Quitting the cycles now outworn,
Let bolder thoughts thy wit engage.
Bring to the gateways of the morn

The broad majestic Period,
That asks his season to be born.
Let faith embrace an ampler God,
Knowledge be rounded to a sphere,

Justice triumphant break her rod.
Recite a lesson more austere,
Which braver bards shall learn to sing,
And braver men shall love to hear.

Far off, too far the Hours that bring
This morrow which we pine to see,
Far off they wait with folded wing.
Yet holy thoughts are prophecy,
The hopeful eye is victory,
The present soul a world to be.